Graceful and Grateful: The Secrets of Women Dancing Through Chaos

Gaudelene Joy Dacuan

Ukiyoto Publishing

All global publishing rights are held by
Ukiyoto Publishing
Published in 2024

Content Copyright © Gaudelene Joy Dacuan

ISBN 9789362696779

All rights reserved.
No part of this publication may be reproduced, transmitted, or stored in a retrieval system, in any form by any means, electronic, mechanical, photocopying, recording or otherwise, without the prior permission of the publisher.

The moral rights of the author have been asserted.

This is a work of fiction. Names, characters, businesses, places, events, locales, and incidents are either the products of the author's imagination or used in a fictitious manner. Any resemblance to actual persons, living or dead, or actual events is purely coincidental.

This book is sold subject to the condition that it shall not by way of trade or otherwise, be lent, resold, hired out or otherwise circulated, without the publisher's prior consent, in any form of binding or cover other than that in which it is published.

www.ukiyoto.com

*I dedicate this book
to the two incredible women
who have been my pillars of strength,
my confidants, and my greatest cheerleaders,
Ate Bel and Ate Cel.*

Contents

Introduction	1
Discovering Grace in Chaos	4
Overcoming Limiting Beliefs	10
Thriving in the Face of Adversity	14
The Dance of Self-Care	19
Cultivating Compassionate Connections	25
Dancing with Gratitude	29
Making a Positive Impact	35
Graceful and Grateful	37
About the Author	*40*

Introduction

Often perceived as unpredictability, chaos harbors a profound role in our personal growth and transformation. Just as turmoil exists in the natural world, it also exists within each person's life through unforeseen challenges, unexpected changes, and moments of upheaval.

Embracing chaos as an inherent part of life's journey allows individuals to break free from stagnant comfort zones and challenge themselves to adapt and evolve. It serves as a catalyst for growth that requires a shift in perspective, seeing it not as a force to be avoided or feared but as an opportunity for self-discovery and expansion.

Instead of succumbing to fear and uncertainty, strong women see chaos as a canvas upon which they can paint their narrative of growth and empowerment. Women who "dance through chaos" know that life's twists and turns are all part of the big picture, and they have learned to move gracefully through these obstacles.

The fact that strong women can dance it out is one of the most potent things they have in common. Instead of having uncertainty take over their lives, they choose to dance to the beat of life, giving them joy and freedom to express themselves. Dancing helps them eliminate stress, feel their emotions, and regain their inner power. Even when they don't know what will happen, they don't hesitate to let their bodies move to the music. They believe that the dance will lead them to the best results. They know that life isn't always what you expect and that trying to control everything can be pointless. Instead, they give in to the current and let it carry them, knowing they can change their steps and respond as needed. By doing this, they open themselves up to new situations and chances they might not have known otherwise.

Gratitude helps women keep a good attitude, even when bad things happen, because it makes them think about what they have instead of what they think they don't have. Their happiness spreads out, making other people want to find joy in their own lives. They become shining examples of hope and strength, telling those around them to face uncertainty with courage and smile. Their contagious energy inspires others to find their interests, go with the flow, and grow thankful hearts.

Ultimately, "Graceful and Grateful: The Secrets of Women Dancing Through Chaos" reveals the empowering philosophy of seeing life as a dance, taking uncertainty with grace, and thriving in the face of chaos. By choosing to dance it out, going with the flow, liking what they do, and cultivating contentment and positivity, these women show how life's challenges can be turned into chances to grow and succeed. May their journey inspire everyone to join the dance of life with joy, resiliency, and thanks because it's in the rhythm of chaos that we find the true meaning of life.

Discovering Grace in Chaos

Chaos could refer to things that make us feel out of control, unstable, or out of our everyday routines. It can come from personal crises, broken dreams, relationship problems, job setbacks, or societal changes. Chaos often makes us feel destructive emotions like stress, worry, and hopelessness, even threatening our physical and mental health. It is undeniably present everywhere in our lives; it shows up as twists and turns that we didn't see coming, testing our sense of security and control.

Chaos upsets the balance we try to keep and makes us feel lost, confused, and defenseless. But did you know that there is room for change and growth, even in chaos? Yes! Despite these times of turmoil, the idea of grace shines through as a leading light.

Grace, for me, has become a beacon of light amid the chaos. A state of inner calm, strength, and acceptance that enables me to rise above the storm. To find grace during the chaos, I discovered several practices that have proven to be invaluable on my journey:

The first is to **cultivate self-awareness**: Self-awareness is essential for finding grace amid chaos. It allows us to recognize and observe our emotions as they arise, allowing us to respond rather than react. It also enables us to take a step back, assess the situation objectively, understand our triggers, and make deliberate choices consistent with our values and philosophies. Furthermore, self-awareness enables us to question negative or self-limiting beliefs, shifting our focus away from chaos and toward potential opportunities for growth and positive change.

Understanding our emotional responses and thought patterns during chaotic times allows us to choose grace over chaos consciously. For example, when faced with a sudden coordinatorship loss at school, I embraced gratitude for the opportunity to explore new paths and grow personally and professionally instead of succumbing to despair and hate against my school head, who removed the coordinatorship from me.

We improve our self-control and reduce impulsive reactions by cultivating self-awareness. We become more aware of our internal state, which allows us to pause, reflect, and respond thoughtfully, even under challenging situations. Finally, self-awareness gives us the tools to stay calm amid chaos, promoting resilience, adaptability, and a graceful approach to life's uncertainties.

The second is to **embrace gratitude**: Finding grace amid chaos is a transformative process that allows us to find meaning and beauty amid complex and turbulent times. Gratitude is essential in this journey because it will enable us to shift our focus from problems to blessings. It's natural for our attention to be drawn to the difficulties, uncertainties, and hardships we face when chaos surrounds us. Gratitude, on the other hand, intentionally redirects our thoughts and emotions toward the positive aspects of our lives.

Practicing gratitude lets us notice small pleasures that go unnoticed during stressful times. It encourages us to take a moment to pause, reflect, and appreciate the moments of beauty, serenity, and goodness that remain. We begin cultivating a positive outlook by acknowledging and being grateful for these small joys, which can counterbalance the negativity and chaos around us. This shift in perspective enables us to find grace even in the most chaotic of situations.

Furthermore, gratitude helps us recognize acts of kindness that occur amid chaos. People often come together to support and uplift one another during difficult times. We become more sensitive to compassion, empathy, and support when we practice gratitude. Recognizing and appreciating these acts of kindness makes us grateful and inspires us to do the same for others. It has a cascading effect of disseminating positivity and grace amid chaos.

Third is to **seek support**: Connecting with loved ones, mentors, or support networks during times of chaos provides a safe space for reflection, guidance, and encouragement. Sharing our burdens and seeking different perspectives can contribute to finding grace within ourselves.

Sharing our struggles and concerns with trusted friends or family fosters a supportive environment where we can express our emotions and thoughts freely. Our loved ones provide a safe space for us to process our experiences through compassionate listening and empathetic responses. Their presence and support remind us that we are not alone in navigating the chaos, which can provide relief and hope.

Mentors offer valuable insights and advice based on their experiences, providing us with guidance and wisdom. Their perspective can shed light on different approaches to the navigation of chaotic situations, assisting us in discovering new solutions and strategies.

Similarly, support networks bring together people who are going through similar experiences. We gain a broader perspective and a sense of solidarity by sharing our experiences and listening to others' stories. This shared understanding can inspire us, boost our resilience, and help us find grace within ourselves.

Becoming more self-aware gives us the power to choose grace over chaos by helping us understand our emotional reactions and thought patterns. It lets us respond with poise and change our points of view. Showing gratitude shifts our attention from our problems to our blessings. It helps us keep a positive attitude by recognizing the small joys, acts of kindness, and lessons learned through hard times. And getting help from loved ones, mentors, or support networks gives us a safe place to think, get advice, and be encouraged. It also lets us share our burdens and see things from different points of view, which helps us find grace within ourselves.

Self-awareness, gratitude, and support put us on a path that changes us and helps us find grace amid chaos, strength, resilience, and inner peace.

Overcoming Limiting Beliefs

In a world where society often sets women's roles and expectations, giving us the tools to break free from these limits is a transformative journey. Step one in this process is to eliminate beliefs that hold us back. We can face these limits we put on ourselves head-on by looking at the power of our stories. This chapter discusses how important it is to challenge social norms, redefine success, and embrace personal journeys. Through this change, we can be freed from the weight of society's expectations and handle chaos with grace.

Every woman has her own story to tell, full of experiences, struggles, and victories. These stories significantly impact how we think and feel about ourselves. By digging into our own stories, we can find the deep-seated beliefs that keep us from moving forward. For example, a woman who grew up thinking she wasn't smart enough because of societal expectations might find out she is astute, challenging the idea that academic success is the only measure of success. By embracing our own stories, we can reclaim our identities and rewrite the stories that have held us back, giving us the power to break out of our limits.

Societal norms often put us under strict rules about how we should act, look, and choose our careers. To eliminate limiting beliefs, we must challenge and change how we think about ourselves. For example, the idea that a woman's worth depends on how she looks can be fought by practicing body positivity and self-acceptance. By questioning the status quo, we can break free from society's expectations and set new standards that align with our identity. Going against social norms opens a world of possibilities and gives us the power to make our paths without worrying about what other people may think.

Society often uses wealth, career success, or social status as success measures. But these narrow definitions must justify the many things we can do. We must let go of the idea that success must fit a specific mold to eliminate limiting beliefs. By redefining success personally, we can embrace a broader range of accomplishments, such as personal growth, nurturing relationships, pursuing passions, or positively impacting our communities.

For example, a woman who puts her mental health ahead of a high-powered career can rethink what success means by finding satisfaction in her inner peace and overall happiness. By accepting that success means different things to different people, we can follow paths that align with our values and goals in life.

Life is often full of chaos, uncertainty, and problems that come up out of the blue. By eliminating limiting beliefs, we can build a strong mindset that gives us the power to handle these challenges gracefully and confidently. By changing our thinking, we can see challenges as chances to grow instead of problems that can't be solved. For example, instead of seeing failure as a sign of our value, we can see it as a step toward success. We learn to adapt, stick with something, and find strength amid chaos by changing how we look at things.

We can explore our untapped potential and become more creative when we change our thinking. We become more willing to take risks, try new things, and go where no one else has before. This newfound strength helps us go beyond what society expects from us.

In conclusion, overcoming limiting beliefs is a powerful journey of self-discovery and empowerment. With our own stories, questioning social norms, redefining success, and making mental shifts, we can dance through chaos without being held back by society's expectations. This change makes it possible for a world where every woman's journey is celebrated, and every woman's full potential is unlocked.

Thriving in the Face of Adversity

Thriving in adversity requires a strong and resilient character for women to overcome challenges and emerge victorious. Here are ten essential characteristics that women must have to succeed in the face of adversity:

Resilience: A resilient woman can bounce back from setbacks, adapt to change, and maintain a positive outlook despite difficult circumstances. When faced with challenges, she views them as opportunities for growth and learning rather than insurmountable obstacles. Her ability to stay strong in adversity inspires those around her. It helps her overcome hurdles and forge a path forward, leading by example with unwavering determination.

Courage: Thriving in adversity demands courage to confront fears, take calculated risks, and step outside one's comfort zone. A courageous woman embraces uncertainty and challenges, knowing that proper growth and achievement lie beyond familiar territories. She recognizes that fear is a natural emotion, but she refuses to let it hold her back from pursuing her dreams and making a positive impact on her life and the lives of others. Her bravery becomes a beacon of hope for others, motivating them to face their fears and strive for their aspirations.

Determination: A determined woman perseveres in the face of obstacles and remains focused on her goals, refusing to give up easily. She possesses an unwavering resolve that propels her forward, no matter how difficult the journey may be. Her tenacity enables her to overcome setbacks and stay committed to her vision, proving that with enough determination, anything is possible. As she achieves her objectives, she inspires those around her to adopt a similar attitude of unwavering dedication.

Resourcefulness: Resourcefulness enables a woman to find creative solutions and maximize limited resources during challenging times. She thinks outside the box when confronted with scarcity or adversity and leverages her ingenuity to overcome obstacles. Her ability to adapt and improvise not only helps her navigate difficult situations but also fosters a sense of confidence and self-reliance. By demonstrating resourcefulness, she empowers others to develop problem-solving skills and discover hidden opportunities in adversity.

Optimism: An optimistic outlook allows women to see the silver lining in difficult situations and maintain hope for a better future. Despite hardships, a spirited woman remains positive, believing that brighter days lie ahead. Her hopeful demeanor guides those around her, providing reassurance and encouragement in times of darkness. By focusing on the potential for positive outcomes, she cultivates resilience and enables herself and others to endure challenges with grace and optimism.

Flexibility: Being flexible and adaptable helps women navigate through ever-changing circumstances and adjust their strategies accordingly. A flexible woman embraces change as an inherent part of life and recognizes that rigidity can hinder progress. She is open to new ideas and perspectives, willing to pivot when necessary to achieve her goals. By displaying flexibility, she encourages those she interacts with to be receptive to change and approach challenges with an adaptable mindset.

Self-belief: Believing in oneself and one's abilities instills the confidence needed to tackle challenges head-on and trust in one's potential for success. A woman with solid self-belief understands her worth and capabilities, enabling her to face adversity with unwavering self-assurance. Her confidence becomes contagious, inspiring others to recognize and embrace their strengths, leading to a collective rise in resilience and determination.

Emotional intelligence: Understanding and managing emotions effectively enables women to stay composed and make sound decisions during adversity. A woman with high emotional intelligence can navigate challenging situations gracefully, maintaining her composure even under pressure. She empathizes with others and cultivates meaningful connections, fostering a supportive environment that encourages collective growth and mutual understanding.

Supportive network: Building a solid support system of friends, family, or mentors provides valuable encouragement and assistance during tough times. A woman with a reliable network can lean on her loved ones for guidance, emotional support, and practical help when facing adversity. This web of support bolsters her resilience and reaffirms her determination to overcome challenges, knowing she is not alone in her journey.

Learning mindset: A woman with a growth mindset embraces adversity as an opportunity to learn and grow, fostering personal development and continuous improvement. She views failures and setbacks as steppingstones toward success, appreciating the valuable lessons they offer. By embracing a learning mindset, she encourages a culture of self-improvement. She inspires those around her to perceive challenges as catalysts for growth, ultimately creating a community of empowered individuals who flourish despite adversity.

With these ten essential characteristics, women are equipped to survive adversity, thrive, and come out stronger on the other side. Together, these characteristics form a formidable arsenal that empowers women to conquer adversity and emerge as stronger, wiser, and more empowered individuals. Their collective strength and resilience inspire others, creating a ripple effect of positive change and progress for women everywhere.

The Dance of Self-Care

Self-care is more than just a buzzword in today's fast-paced and demanding world. It has become an essential practice for all of us who want to find balance, well-being, and inner peace. Through the transformative dance of self-care, we have learned how important it is to put ourselves first. We know how to set limits, deal with stress, and form healthy habits that are good for our mind, body, and soul. By making self-care a core part of our lives, we gain the energy and strength we need to handle life's challenges gracefully and effortlessly.

Creativity and personal growth are essential parts of the magical world of self-care. We can be ourselves and use our natural talents and passions when we take part in creative activities. Creativity becomes a safe place for self-discovery and self-expression through painting, writing, dancing, or something else. This process of exploring helps us grow and gives us a deep sense of happiness and fulfillment.

By combining self-care with creativity, we can start a fantastic journey of self-discovery where we learn to honor our needs, develop self-compassion, and embrace our unique identities. This dance helps us find our authentic voices and break free from society's expectations. In the end, self-care becomes a powerful tool that helps us live happier, more balanced, and more purposeful lives.

Setting limits in any relationship is also essential for keeping things healthy. Just like dance partners who need clear cues and personal space to move together well, they must set boundaries to ensure they respect each other and are emotionally healthy. This means being clear with others about what we want, need, and limits. Doing this builds stronger relationships; eventually, we will feel understood, valued, and supported. This creates a dance of harmony and balance in relationships with the people around us.

Setting limits is also an essential skill in the workplace. At work, it's easy for demands and responsibilities to become too much, which can cause stress and dissatisfaction. By setting clear boundaries, we can have a healthy work-life balance and keep work from taking over their time and health. Limiting our time and energy can make our workplaces more productive and satisfying while protecting our mental and physical health.

Ultimately, taking care of ourselves and setting limits go hand in hand. Setting boundaries helps us take charge of our lives, put our well-being first, and build healthy relationships, just like a dancer's graceful movements do. Edges give us the structure and balance we need to do well in our personal, professional, and family lives. By embracing the dance of self-care and substantially setting boundaries, we can create a fulfilling and harmonious life with our needs and values.

We can find harmony during life's challenges by using techniques like deep breathing, mindfulness, and meditation, being physically active, eating a balanced diet, and keeping social connections. The dance of self-care helps us deal with stress with grace, resilience, and a renewed sense of fulfillment. This, in turn, leads to a more balanced and fulfilling life.

People often talk about how important it is to be mentally and emotionally healthy. Mindfulness and meditation help us become more self-aware, which allows us to deal with stress and anxiety more effectively. By recognizing and dealing with our emotions, we can keep our minds and bodies in balance and harmony, which helps us have a favorable view of life.

We should also be aware that self-care isn't just about caring for ourselves but also about caring for others and the environment. Kindness, empathy, and caring for the environment all help make the world more caring and connected. And we play a big part in making the world a healthier and happier place.

Developing healthy habits is essential to women's self-care, including our physical, mental, and emotional health. Crucial aspects of this journey are doing things that bring us joy and satisfaction, practicing mindfulness, and building a supportive community. Also, our commitment to taking care of ourselves, others, and the environment has a ripple effect that makes the world kinder and more peaceful. By learning the dance of self-care, we can live good lives for ourselves and those around us.

The dance of self-care is a beautiful and empowering journey that puts us at the center of our lives, radiating the essence of self-love and nourishment. Setting limits becomes a graceful dance that helps us protect our emotional and mental safe spaces while making our relationships with other people healthier. Taking care of stress becomes a skillful pas de deux with life's challenges, letting us handle even the trickiest steps with poise and confidence. As we develop healthy habits, like caring for our bodies and minds with mindfulness and compassion, the dance becomes a vibrant symphony of personal growth and change.

In this dance of self-care, we find the harmony that lives in our souls. This helps us develop a deep and satisfying relationship with ourselves. As we make self-care a regular part of our lives, how we move becomes a rhythm of well-being that others around us can feel. We become sources of strength and inspiration for others, encouraging them to go on their journeys of self-discovery and growth. This symphony of self-care changes people's lives and makes the world a more compassionate, empathetic, and understanding place. So, when the music in their hearts starts playing, the stage is set with intention, and the dance of self-care begins, each of us becomes the star of our unique and enchanting show.

With each step we take in the name of self-love, we celebrate our beauty and worth, showing how beautiful it is to be vulnerable and strong. We find freedom through the dance of self-care. As we care for our minds, bodies, and souls with grace and love, we can enjoy the brilliance of who we are.

Cultivating Compassionate Connections

In our fast-paced, connected world, genuine and caring relationships with others are more critical than ever. This chapter looks at our unique path as we realize how powerful it is to build relationships with people we care about. Empathy and understanding are the building blocks that help us handle the ups and downs of life with grace. Healthy relationships give us a sense of support, encouragement, and belonging. As we explore compassionate connections, we find that it dramatically affects our lives, helping us deal with problems, celebrate successes, and bond with others.

For most of us, making caring connections is very important and has much meaning. It gives us the tools to find strength in vulnerability, understand how others feel, and build a strong sense of community. These connections go beyond being acquaintances and lead to friendships and networks that helps each other. As we share our happiness and sadness, hopes and dreams, we build a web of strength that allows us to move through the different stages of life. By encouraging empathy and understanding, we better understand how other people's lives are. This helps break down barriers and create a sense of unity among people from different backgrounds. In the end, embracing the power of compassionate connections improves our lives, allowing us to thrive, inspire, and make positive changes in our communities and the world.

Compassionate connections go beyond small talk and create an environment where people can trust and help each other. The effects of compassionate connections go beyond the people involved. As more we treat each other with kindness and understanding, we set an excellent example for others to follow. Growing compassionate connections makes society as a whole more empathetic and caring. People become more sensitive to each other's needs, bridging gaps, and fostering a sense of unity and shared humanity.

In our search for caring relationships, we find strength, encouragement, and a sense of belonging in supportive relationships. During hard times, spending time with people who share our interests or have been through similar things can be helpful.

This supportive setting lets us break free from society's rules and be ourselves without worrying about being judged. Through shared experiences, we feel validated and empowered, which can change our personal and professional lives.

Yes! Compassionate connections also affect both personal and professional settings. A compassionate leader at work can make the team environment more welcoming and supportive. Employees feel valued and appreciated, making them happier and more productive at work. These leaders make others more caring, which starts a positive cycle that helps the whole organization.

In conclusion, empathy and genuine understanding are at the heart of compassionate connections. As we embrace and care for these connections, we strengthen our relationships and help build a society with more compassion and empathy. We can make more profound and meaningful connections with each other and their communities by giving support, actively listening, and recognizing emotions without passing judgment. Compassionate relationships make the world peaceful, where empathy is the key to growth, understanding, and well-being.

To keep building empathy, women can keep learning and getting to know people with different points of view. This could mean going to workshops, reading books from other cultures, or actively looking for new things to do. By seeing more of the world, women can learn more about other people's struggles and successes, making them more empathetic and understanding.

Dancing with Gratitude

Gratitude is frequently viewed as a static emotion, a moment of thanksgiving for the good things in life. What if we saw gratitude as a dynamic, ever-present dance? In this chapter, we will look at the concept of dancing with gratitude and how it can help us navigate life's chaos.

Gratitude is more than simply saying "thank you." It is an attitude, a way of viewing the world that recognizes the beauty and blessings that surround us, even in the midst of adversity. At its core, gratitude is a profound recognition of the good in our lives, regardless of the difficulties we face. It invites us to pause and reflect on the small, often overlooked moments of joy and wonder that fill our lives. By cultivating this mindful awareness, we can learn to appreciate the warmth of the morning sun, the kindness of a stranger, or the simple pleasure of laughing with a friend. These fleeting moments enrich our lives and provide a steadying presence amidst life's uncertainties.

Furthermore, gratitude shifts our perspective, allowing us to see silver linings where we would otherwise only see clouds. When we adopt a grateful mindset, we shift our focus from what is lacking to what is abundant, turning setbacks into opportunities for growth. This shift in perspective not only improves our emotional well-being, but it also fosters resilience, allowing us to navigate life's inevitable challenges with greater grace and poise. Embracing gratitude does not imply ignoring our challenges; rather, it prepares us to face them with a fortified spirit, finding strength and hope in the recognition of life's intrinsic goodness.

One of the most important advantages of gratitude is its ability to promote emotional resilience. When we recognize and appreciate the positives, we improve our ability to deal with stress and overcome adversity. Gratitude acts as a buffer, mitigating the effects of negative emotions and encouraging a more balanced outlook on life. This resilience allows us to face challenges with confidence and optimism, knowing that there is always something to be grateful for, even in difficult times.

Expressing gratitude strengthens our connections with others, which improves our relationships.

When we take the time to acknowledge and appreciate the contributions of those around us, we foster mutual respect and strengthen our relationships. This positive reinforcement builds a support network that can help us get through difficult times. By fostering gratitude in our interactions, we create a caring and supportive community, making it easier to face life's challenges together.

Regular gratitude can also have a significant impact on our mental health. It has been shown to alleviate symptoms of depression and anxiety by promoting a positive attitude and feelings of happiness and fulfillment. When we concentrate on what we are grateful for, we can relieve the weight of our worries and cultivate a sense of calm. This mental clarity enables us to approach life with a more balanced and joyful mindset, thereby improving our overall quality of life.

Furthermore, gratitude promotes physical health benefits, which lead to a healthier and more vibrant life. Studies have shown that gratitude can improve sleep, lower blood pressure, and boost the immune system. Gratitude improves our physical well-being by lowering stress and encouraging a positive outlook, leaving us feeling more energized and capable. This holistic approach to health emphasizes the value of gratitude as an essential component of a fulfilling and healthy lifestyle.

Incorporating gratitude into your life is similar to learning a dance: it takes practice, mindfulness, and a willingness to be present. Daily reflection is a foundational step in this dance. Begin or end your day by thinking about three things you're grateful for. This simple practice can either set a positive tone for the day or provide a sense of closure and peace before bedtime. Making this a daily habit trains your mind to focus on the positive aspects of your life, cultivating a more optimistic outlook and mitigating the effects of stress.

Maintaining a gratitude journal is another effective method for cultivating gratitude. Keep track of your daily reflections, including both significant events and small moments of joy. Over time, this journal will serve as a valuable reminder of the good in your life, particularly during difficult times. Writing down your thoughts promotes deeper reflection and reinforces the habit of recognizing and appreciating positive experiences. Reviewing your journal entries can provide comfort and perspective by reminding you of the abundance in your life, even when times are difficult.

Mindful moments throughout the day can also help you develop your gratitude practice. Take a moment to appreciate your surroundings, whether it's the beauty of nature, the warmth of a cup of coffee, or a thoughtful gesture from a coworker. Recognizing these moments and allowing them to fill you with gratitude can significantly boost your overall well-being. This mindfulness practice helps you stay in the present moment, reducing anxiety about the future and regrets about the past while allowing you to fully experience and appreciate the here and now.

Thanking those around you is another important aspect of dancing with gratitude. Make it a habit to express gratitude through words, notes, or simple acts of kindness. This not only creates a positive environment, but it also improves your relationships. When you express gratitude on a regular basis, you foster an environment of appreciation that benefits everyone involved. Incorporating gratitude habits into your daily routine, such as sharing what each family member is grateful for at dinner or engaging in a personal meditation practice, helps to reinforce this positive attitude. These habits help to weave gratitude into the fabric of your daily life, making it a natural and integral part of your interactions with the world. Finally, when faced with a challenge, look for the brighter side. Consider what you can learn from the situation and what positive outcomes may occur. This shift in perspective can turn challenges into opportunities for growth, transforming adversity into a dance of resilience and appreciation.

Finally, dancing with gratitude is about approaching life with an open heart. It's about finding beauty in the chaos and grace in the adversity. We can transform our lives by cultivating a gratitude mindset, which promotes resilience, joy, and deeper connections with ourselves and others. Let us remember that gratitude is more than just a reaction to good times; it is a companion through all of life's ups and downs. Let us dance with it and allow it to guide us through the chaos.

Making a Positive Impact

Our presence as women exudes a profound sense of resilience and compassion in a world that grapples with challenges and uncertainties. This chapter explores these virtues' importance, focusing on how we can make a difference in our communities. It celebrates the power of our voices and stories to change people's lives.

Our voices are one of the most powerful assets we have. Every person has a unique point of view shaped by their experiences, struggles, and successes. By courageously telling these stories, we break down isolation barriers and give hope to people going through their hard times. When we share hope, we start a beautiful chain reaction that gives others power and leads to lasting change.

But we don't just make a difference by telling stories; our actions and initiatives are also significant. We are at the forefront of community-building projects, advocacy campaigns, and charitable efforts, all of which aim to help others and build hope for the future. Our commitment to giving power to the weak, assisting people to get an education, and fighting for justice shows that we always try to improve the world.

Also, the effects of our actions go beyond one person's empowerment. By encouraging other people to find their ways to happiness and success, we set off a chain reaction that speeds up progress on a larger scale. Because people are connected, empathy and compassion grow, creating a place where people can change and grow.

Spreading hope and love isn't just something we do once; it's something we do all the time. It takes courage, determination, and a strong belief that things can improve. It recognizes that progress isn't always a straight line and spreading hope and love makes the world better.

In conclusion, making a positive difference by spreading hope and love is vital to making society fairer and more peaceful. We have a fantastic ability to inspire, uplift, and empower others through our voices and stories. We started a chain reaction of empowerment and progress that went far beyond our lives by spreading hope and love. Let's honor what we did and answer the call to make the world full of hope, love, and compassion.

Graceful and Grateful

In a chaotic and unforgiving world, women have become shining examples of grace and gratitude. We have a fantastic ability to navigate the rough seas of life with strength and poise. Our secret is that we embrace our inner dance, a metaphor for our strength and ability to change. This allows us to dance gracefully through storms.

Dancing through chaos with grace and gratitude is not a one-time accomplishment but a process of growth and self-discovery that lasts a lifetime. Women constantly change, learn, and adapt, like a dance that changes and shifts with every step. Embracing this fluidity gives us the confidence and calmness to face challenges, even in the worst storms.

This inner dance starts with taking care of ourselves. We often take care of other people and put our own needs last. But if we take the time to care for ourselves physically, emotionally, and mentally, we can get our energy back and be even better caregivers and support systems for our families and communities.

Our relationships are also a big part of how we can dance through chaos. A sense of security and belonging comes from solid relationships with people we care about. When things are hard, these relationships act as a safety net by giving support, understanding, and love. We get strength from these connections, which help us find comfort in hard times and keep going.

Gratitude helps us shift our attention from what we don't have to what we do have. This helps us keep a positive attitude and find beauty and joy even when things are hard. By noticing the good things in our lives, we develop a deep appreciation for the little things that make us happy. This makes the journey through chaos more meaningful and rewarding.

With our newfound strength and thankfulness, we become lights of hope for other people. As we talk about how we overcame hard times and found strength, we give others the courage to dance through chaos gracefully. This creates a chain of empowerment, where the flame of resilience is passed from one woman to the next, making a group of women who help and support each other.

In a world where hatred and discord are common, the dance of grace and gratitude can be a powerful force for good. When we dance through chaos with resilience and gratitude, we improve our health and help create a world where compassion, empathy, and love are the most important things. Our actions set the stage for a society that welcomes differences, tries to understand others, and looks for ways to come together.

Ultimately, the fact that we, women, can dance through chaos with grace and gratitude shows our strength. As we continue to embrace our inner dance, take care of ourselves and our relationships, and give hope to others, we become guiding lights in a world that often seems dark and tumultuous. Our unwavering strength and determination inspire others to do the same, making the world a better place with less hate and more kindness. Let's celebrate our ability to dance amid chaos, and may our stories continue to spark hope in everyone.

About the Author

Gaudelene Joy N. Dacuan

Gaudelene Joy is a recipient of several awards as an educator, dancer, graphic designer, academic and sports coach, and celebrated as an international award-winning author and researcher. She is a public school teacher and a philomath who believes in the beauty of having a little knowledge about everything, and uses it to inspire and empower learners of all ages through her writings.

www.ingramcontent.com/pod-product-compliance
Lightning Source LLC
LaVergne TN
LVHW041557070526
838199LV00046B/2022